This book belongs to:

....

MR. MEN
and
LITTLE MISS
CHRISTMAS TREASURY

Roger Hargreaves

A treasury of 10 magical Christmas tales from
the Mr. Men and Little Miss Story Collection

EGMONT

We bring stories to life

MR. MEN LITTLE MISS
MR. MEN™ LITTLE MISS™ © THOIP (a Sanrio company)

Mr. Men and Little Miss Christmas Treasury © 2013 THOIP (a Sanrio company).
Printed and published under licence from Price Stern Sloan, Inc., Los Angeles.
First published in Great Britain 2013 by Egmont UK Limited
The Yellow Building, 1 Nicholas Road, London W11 4AN

ISBN 978 1 4052 6595 9
54025/1
Printed in China

CONTENTS

MR. CHRISTMAS

In my snow-covered cottage at the South Pole I was having breakfast.

Christmas Pudding!

That frosty morning, as I was popping the last piece of marmalade-covered plum pudding into my mouth, there was a knock on the door of Mistletoe Cottage.

When I opened the door, I saw that it was the postman.

"Hello, Percy," I said. "Come on in out of the cold."

"Don't mind if I do," replied Percy. "There's a bit of a nip in the air today."

"I've got a letter for you," said Percy. "And as it has a North Pole postmark, I suppose it's from your uncle."

Everybody at the South Pole knows about my famous uncle who lives at the North Pole.

"Good old Father Christmas," I chuckled. "Haven't heard from him for ages!"

"Well," remarked Percy, "thanks for the warm-up. I had better be off now."

I opened the envelope.

"Dear Nephew," read the letter, "I hope all is well down there. We are busy as usual up here, getting things organised for Christmas. Which is one of the reasons I am writing to you.

"Can you help?

"Each year I am finding it more and more difficult to get round all those Mr Men! There seem to be so many of them all over the place, and I was wondering if, this year, as a big favour to your old uncle, you could stand in for me?

"Hoping you can help. Your ever loving uncle."

That very evening I put through a long distance call to North Pole 253.

"Hello?" chuckled a rather deep, rumbly voice at the other end of the telephone, "Father Christmas speaking!"

"Hello Uncle," I said. "Your letter arrived this morning, and I'd love to help!"

"Oh good for you," the voice rumbled in my ear. "If you have a pencil and paper, I'll give you the Mr Men's names and addresses."

"I'd no idea there were so many of them," I said.

"Do you think you can manage?" asked my famous uncle. "I'll lend you a couple of reindeer if you like."

"Oh no," I said. "I can manage."

I read through the list of Mr Men while I was having supper.

"This is going to keep me busy," I said. "First things first,"
I thought to myself. "And the first thing I need is transport!"

"And the first thing to do if I need transport," I thought as I chewed,
"is to talk to the Wizard!"

Wizard Winterbottom!

The following morning, I set off to see the Wizard.

It had been snowing again during the night, and I was quite out of breath by the time I arrived at Wizard Winterbottom's castle.

I must say it's the biggest castle I've ever seen.

Mind you, it has to be big, because Wizard Winterbottom is a giant.

And there, goodness knows how many times taller than me, stood the huge figure of Wizard Winterbottom.

"Christmas!" he boomed in a voice that made my head spin. "How nice to see you! Come in! Follow me!"

"Now," thundered Wizard Winterbottom. "What brings you here on a cold winter's morning like this?"

I told him all about my famous uncle, and all about how I'd been asked to help, and all about the Mr Men, and all about where they lived, and all about the fact that I needed transport. Special transport!

"Can you help me?" I asked hopefully.

"Hmmm ... yes," he said eventually. "But I can't do anything until next week!"

"Thank you very much," I replied.

"Goodbye!" I shouted, but he didn't hear me, he was already too busy thinking.

Exactly two weeks later I paid a return visit to the enormous castle.

"Hello, Christmas," boomed the giant voice.

He took me into his kitchen, lifted me up on to his enormous table, and set me down with a bit of a bump.

"There's your transport," said Wizard Winterbottom.

"But that's your teapot!" I said in bewilderment.

"You're looking at the world's first flying teapot!" he laughed. "It's fuelled by teabags. I've put an engine inside the spout! All you do is refuel every thousand miles, and you can fly at up to three times the speed of sound!"

We took the Flying Teapot outside the castle, and I pressed the start button in great excitement.

I zoomed right around the South Pole in no time at all, and landed safely back at the castle.

"Well?" asked Wizard Winterbottom.

I was lost for words.

"Fanjollytastic?" suggested the wizard.

I grinned. "Absojollylutely," I replied.

That evening, I sat down and made a list of Christmas presents for all the Mr Men.

Another list.

A very long list.

I didn't finish until three o'clock in the morning!

I spent the next week and a half wrapping up all the presents, and almost before I knew it, December 24th arrived.

Christmas Eve!

"It's going to be a long day," I thought to myself as I packed all the brightly coloured parcels into my Flying Teapot.

It was snowing lightly as I took off from the South Pole.

That Christmas Eve was indeed a very long day, and a very long night too.

And the moon was just disappearing over the horizon of Loudland when I delivered the last of the presents to Mr Quiet.

I was quite exhausted.

Christmas morning dawned, and all over the world everyone started
to open their presents.

At seven o'clock Mr Fussy opened his present. Three hundred and sixty five yellow dusters. One for every day of the year!

At five past seven Mr Small opened his present. One jelly bean! Gift wrapped. Banana flavoured. A feast!

At ten past seven Mr Greedy opened his present. A cookery book entitled: 1001 WAYS TO ROAST AN OX! Mr Greedy licked his lips and rubbed his tummy.

At quarter past seven Mr Tall opened his present. Socks. Striped socks.
The longest, stripiest pair of stretchy socks you've ever seen!

At twenty past seven Mr Muddle opened a packet of cornflakes.
"Funny sort of present," he thought to himself, not noticing his real present.

At twenty-five past seven Mr Mean opened his present. A purse. A very,
very small purse. Just small enough not to take any money!

At half past seven Mr Forgetful opened his present.
"Is it my birthday?" he thought to himself.

At twenty to eight Mr Chatterbox opened his present. A dictionary.
"How very very very very very very very very useful," he murmured.

At a quarter to eight Mr Topsy-Turvy opened his present. A picture.
"How nice," he said as he hung it on the wall. Upside down!

At ten to eight Mr Uppity opened his present.
A present for the man who has everything.
A gold-plated backscratcher!

At five to eight Mr Funny opened his present.
A book of knock knock jokes.
Knock-knock! Who's there? You know the sort of thing.

And, at eight o'clock precisely, Mr Silly opened his present.
An electric, fully automatic, instant, digital, computerised Thingumajig!

What's an electric, fully automatic, instant, digital, computerised Thingumajig?

I've no idea!

Just after eight o'clock that Christmas morning the telephone rang.

"Hello," I answered. "Happy Christmas!"

"That's me," laughed Father Christmas on the other end. "And a happy Christmas to you too.

"How did it go?" Father Christmas asked me.

"Just got back," I said.

"Me too," sighed my uncle wearily. "Had a bit of a problem in France," he added. "Got stuck in a chimney."

"It's all those mince pies," I chuckled.

And that is the end of my story.

Well.

Nearly.

Almost.

Not quite.

At five o'clock in the afternoon Mr Slow finally managed to open his present.

Five o'clock in the afternoon was the time.

And the day?

New Year's Eve!

LITTLE MISS CHRISTMAS

Little Miss Christmas lives in an igloo at the North Pole, next door to her uncle, Father Christmas, a long, long way from her brother, Mr Christmas.

Little Miss Christmas works for Father Christmas.

Her job is wrapping all the presents before Father Christmas delivers them on Christmas Eve.

As you might imagine, there are an awful lot of presents to wrap – it takes her all year long. And as much as Little Miss Christmas loves her job, there are times when wrapping presents day in and day out can get a bit boring.

Last year, after nearly a whole year buried in wrapping paper and sticky tape, Little Miss Christmas decided that she deserved a holiday.

She had nearly finished wrapping all the presents, and thought that it would not do any harm for Father Christmas to wrap the last few himself.

To make it easier for him, she rang her brother at the South Pole and asked him to come and help.

Mr Christmas flew up to the North Pole in his magic, flying teapot on the day Little Miss Christmas left for her holiday.

"I won't be back until the day before Christmas Eve, so you have to make sure you finish wrapping the last of the presents," Little Miss Christmas reminded them just before she boarded her plane.

"Don't worry," boomed Father Christmas. "We've got plenty of time! We'll have them all wrapped long before you return."

The next morning, after a breakfast of Christmas pudding on toast, Father Christmas led Mr Christmas into the wrapping room and they set to work.

"This isn't going to take any time at all," said Father Christmas an hour later. "In fact, we've got plenty of time left. How about a game of golf?"

"Good idea," said Mr Christmas.

And so the two of them played golf for the rest of the day.

The following morning, they settled down to work. But after an hour, Father Christmas piped up again, "How do you fancy going reindeer racing? We've got plenty of time left to do this."

"Good idea," agreed Mr Christmas.

And the two of them spent the rest of the day racing reindeer across the ice.

The next day, they did not even reach the wrapping room.

"We've still got plenty of time to finish that wrapping. Shall we go fishing today?" suggested Father Christmas at breakfast.

"Good idea," said Mr Christmas, eagerly.

And so it continued.

While Little Miss Christmas lay on a beach in the Christmas Islands (where else?!), blissfully unaware of what was going on, Father Christmas and Mr Christmas were spending a lot of time having fun and very little time wrapping presents.

So you will not be surprised to learn that the wrapping had not been finished by the time Little Miss Christmas returned from her holiday.

"What have you two been doing all this time?" exclaimed Little Miss Christmas, when she saw the huge pile of unwrapped presents.

Father Christmas and Mr Christmas sheepishly studied their feet, unable to look Little Miss Christmas in the eye.

"How are we ever going to get all this done by tomorrow evening?" she continued, angrily.

It was then that she suddenly had an idea.

A brilliant idea.

"We can ask all the Mr Men and Little Misses to help us! And you can go and pick them up in your teapot!" she cried, pointing at Mr Christmas.

By teatime, Mr Christmas had collected as many of the Mr Men and Little Misses as he could find, and brought them to the North Pole.

They all worked right through the night, although Little Miss Christmas had
to be careful about which jobs she gave them.

Mr Bump was only allowed to wrap teddy bears because he kept breaking
the other presents he was given.

And Little Miss Bossy had to keep a careful eye on Little Miss Naughty,
to stop her wrapping nasty surprises in her presents.

Not everything quite went to plan.

Mr Muddle kept writing "Happy Easter" on the labels.

And Little Miss Helpful tried very hard to be helpful, but got into a lot of trouble with the sticky tape.

Mr Forgetful kept forgetting to put presents in his parcels.

And there was no mistaking the presents wrapped by Mr Messy!

However, by lunch time on Christmas Eve, all the presents were wrapped and labelled and packed away in Father Christmas's sleigh.

"Thank you so much," said Little Miss Christmas to everyone. "I don't know what we would have done without your help. There would have been a lot of empty spaces under a lot of Christmas trees. Now we just need Father Christmas! Has anyone seen him?"

But nobody had.

Eventually, Little Miss Christmas found him playing cards – with Mr Christmas, of course!

"Quick, quick!" she cried. "You're going to be late!"

"Don't worry, don't worry," chuckled Father Christmas.

"We've got plenty of time!"

MR. SNOW

One night, two days before Christmas, it started to snow.

All night it snowed and snowed and snowed and snowed and snowed.

Millions and billions and trillions of big, white, soft snowflakes covered the whole wide world.

When morning came, it was quite amazing to see just how much snow had fallen.

All the houses, all the trees, all the roads and all the fields were covered.

It was almost as if a huge white blanket had been gently laid over everything.

Everywhere you looked was white!

And then the sun came out!

And so did the children!

They were all dressed up and muffled up, wearing scarves and woollies and gloves and boots so that they wouldn't catch cold.

All the children were so excited to see so much snow, which isn't surprising really because there was more snow than they'd ever seen before.

Some of them went on their sledges, racing down the hills.

Some of them who didn't have sledges threw snowballs at each other.

One little boy even made a snowball that was as big as himself.

And some of the children made snowmen!

Then it was Christmas Eve.

The children all went home early so that they could go to bed early so that they could get up early to see what Father Christmas had brought them.

But that particular Christmas Eve, Father Christmas was in trouble.

And the trouble was that it had snowed so much that Father Christmas was stuck.

Well and truly stuck!

There was so much snow that his reindeer simply couldn't pull his sleigh piled high with all the presents that he had to deliver to all the children.

"Oh dear!" thought Father Christmas to himself. "Oh dear me. What am I to do?"

He sat down on his sack of toys and thought and thought how he could manage to deliver all the presents to all the children before they woke up on Christmas morning.

"Oh dear! Oh dear me!" he said out loud, and sighed.

Now, it just so happened that Father Christmas had got himself stuck just beside a snowman which one of the children had built.

And that gave him an idea.

A good idea.

A very good idea.

A very good idea indeed.

"How would you like to help me?" he asked the snowman.

But of course the snowman didn't answer because snowmen can't talk, can they?

"Of course, I'll have to use some of my magic to bring him to life," thought Father Christmas to himself.

So he tugged his white beard three times and muttered some Father Christmassy magic words into it.

Suddenly, you might almost say magically, the snowman did come to life.

"Hello, Father Christmas," said Mr Snow, which was the snowman's name.

"You look a bit sort of stuck if you ask me, which you aren't, but I'll say so anyway, and if you ask me again I'd say you need a sort of helping hand, if you know what I mean, which you probably do, because that's probably why you've brought me to life, which you certainly did, so can I be of any assistance?"

Mr Snow, as you might have gathered, was a rather talkative sort of a snowman.

"Exactly!" beamed Father Christmas. "Let's get started!"

And start they did.

Mr Snow gave Father Christmas an enormous push, and off they went.

They divided the work between them.

It was Mr Snow's job to make sure that all the right toys for all the right boys, and all the right toys for all the right girls, were put into all the right sacks.

It was Father Christmas's job to make sure he took all the right sacks down all the right chimneys and delivered all the right toys to all the right boys and all the right toys to all the right girls.

Mr Snow and Father Christmas made sure that Susan got her teddy bear.

Mr Snow and Father Christmas made sure that Peter got his train.

Mr Snow and Father Christmas made sure that John got his piggy bank.

Mr Snow and Father Christmas even made sure that little Jane got her squeaky pink elephant to play with in the bath.

And then, all of a sudden, they discovered that, between them, they'd finished.

"I'd like to thank you very much indeed for helping me deliver all the right toys to all the right boys," said Father Christmas, shaking Mr Snow by the hand.

"Not forgetting all the right toys to all the right girls," replied Mr Snow, shaking Father Christmas by the hand.

"And now I'd better turn you back into a snowman again," said Father Christmas.

"Thank you again and goodbye!"

"My pleasure!" smiled Mr Snow.

And do you know, from that Christmas to this Christmas, Father Christmas always chooses a snowman to help him.

So, the next time you build a snowman, you'd better make sure you build him properly, because somebody you know might want that snowman to give him a hand.

And you know who that would be, don't you?

MR. MEN
A Christmas Carol

Does Mr Mean have any money?

He has pots of it!

And he keeps it all hidden under his floorboards.

But does Mr Mean spend any of his money?

Hardly a penny!

Guess what Mr Mean has for every meal?

A can of baked beans.

A can of cold baked beans because he is too mean to turn the cooker on!

Now, I am sure you are wondering how Mr Mean makes all his money.

He owns a factory that makes piggy banks.

And because Mr Mean is so mean he pays his staff hardly any money at all.

And they only get one day off a year! Christmas Day. Mr Mean considers this to be far too much time off!

If anyone complains, then Mr Mean points out his best worker, who has worked for him the longest, who has never complained and who always has a smile for his boss.

"Look at Mr Happy," says Mr Mean. "He works for me and he's happy!"

Late on Christmas Eve, after everyone but Mr Mean and Mr Happy had gone home, the factory received a visitor. It was Little Miss Sunshine. She was there to invite the two of them to Christmas lunch the following day.

"Christmas lunch!" spluttered Mr Mean. "What a lot of stuff and nonsense! Before I know it, you'll be expecting me to buy presents for everyone! **Humbug!**"

"How about you, Mr Happy?" asked Little Miss Sunshine, ignoring Mr Mean's outburst. "Would you like to come?"

"Oh . . . Oh I . . . I won't be able to make it," said Mr Happy. "But thank you for asking me."

"Never mind," said Little Miss Sunshine. "Have a good day and Happy Christmas to you both!"

"Bah, humbug," muttered Mr Mean, as he sat counting his money.

On his way home, Mr Happy looked in the shop windows.

"I wish I could go to Little Miss Sunshine's Christmas lunch,"
he murmured to himself, as he gazed at a bright window display full
of presents. "But how can I possibly go when I cannot afford to take
presents for everyone?"

With a heavy sigh, Mr Happy glumly trudged through the snow.

That evening, Mr Mean only had half a tin of cold baked beans because his factory was going to be closed for a whole day.

It was very cold in his house, but rather than light a fire, he went to bed.

Mr Mean counts coins rather than sheep to get himself to sleep. And while he slept, Mr Mean dreamed a very strange and troubling dream in which he met three people.

The first person he met was Mr Nosey, who showed Mr Mean what his past Christmas Day had been like.

Mr Mean saw himself sitting all alone. No friends, no presents, no comfortable fire and no Christmas lunch. And then Mr Mean saw everyone else enjoying themselves.

Mr Mean groaned in his sleep and turned restlessly under his thin blanket.

The next person to visit Mr Mean's dream was Little Miss Wise, and she showed him what the present Christmas Day was going to be like.

Mr Mean saw Mr Happy sitting alone and cold in his house eating a can of cold baked beans. And he doesn't even like baked beans. He was too poor to heat his house and too embarrassed to go to Little Miss Sunshine's house without presents for everyone.

"He doesn't look very happy, does he?" observed Little Miss Wise. "Not so much Mr Happy, more like Mr Sad."

Mr Mean moaned in his sleep and clutched his flat pillow.

The third person to appear in his dream was Little Miss Bossy. She showed Mr Mean what his future Christmases had in store.

A miserable-looking Mr Happy walked through the Town, and as this sad person greeted the people he met in the street, Mr Mean noticed something.

"Everyone is calling him Mr Sad!" exclaimed Mr Mean.

"That's because he is," explained Little Miss Bossy. "He isn't happy anymore so now everyone calls him Mr Sad. And that . . . is all your fault!"

With these words ringing in his ears, Mr Mean woke up with a start.

Sunlight was streaming into his cottage as he jumped out of bed.

"Oh my, oh my!" he cried as he rushed out of the door.

In a great flurry of activity, Mr Mean ran from shop to shop, pounding on doors and making the shopkeepers open up their shops for him.

Mr Happy was just getting up when he heard a loud knocking at his door. He could not believe his eyes when he opened it. Nor his ears.

"HAPPY CHRISTMAS!" cried Mr Mean. "No time to waste. Quick, quick, we're off to Little Miss Sunshine's!"

"But I can't go," blurted out Mr Happy. "I don't have any presents!"

"All taken care of!" cried Mr Mean.

And do you know what?

He was right. Behind him on the snowy path was a sledge laden with brightly wrapped presents.

Little Miss Sunshine was overjoyed to see the two of them.

Mr Happy and Mr Mean (rather to his surprise) had a wonderful day. Lots of friends, presents, a warm fire and a huge Christmas lunch.

"I couldn't ask for anything more," said Mr Happy. "Thank you, Mr Mean."

"You might not ask for anything more, but you're going to get it," said Mr Mean, and with this he gave Mr Happy a present. "It's just something to remember me by."

Mr Happy opened the present.

It was a tin of **baked beans!**

MR. MEN

The Night Before Christmas

It was the night before Christmas, Christmas Eve, and everyone was prepared for Christmas Day.

Everyone except for Mr Wrong, who thought it was the night before his holiday.

All the Mr Men had decorated their Christmas trees, except for
Mr Muddle who had decorated himself.

And everyone had sent their letter to Father Christmas in good time, except for Little Miss Late who had only sent her letter that morning.

Would it get to Father Christmas in time?

In each house, the Christmas cakes were baked.

Mr Greedy had sensibly baked three. One for Christmas Eve and one for Christmas Day. And one because you never know when you might feel peckish.

In each house, the stockings were hung by the chimney, in the hope that Father Christmas would soon be there.

Mr Small was not entirely sure it was fair that you had to hang up your own stocking.

And in each house, the presents were wrapped.

Little Miss Naughty's friends were in for quite a surprise!

The carol singers had sung at each house.

Mr Noisy had loosened some tiles with his 'Ding Dong Merrily on High'!

At the North Pole, Little Miss Christmas had wrapped presents
from dawn to dusk, but finally the sleigh was packed.

Father Christmas and Mr Christmas sneaked in a quick cup of tea, waved goodbye to Little Miss Christmas, and then they were away.

But would they stop at Little Miss Late's house?

It was the night before Christmas, and all through the land not a Mr Man was stirring, not even Little Miss Chatterbox. They were all dreaming about a visit from Father Christmas.

Mr Greedy was nestled all snug in his bed with visions of turkey and sprouts dancing in his head!

Everybody was fast asleep. Everybody?

Well, not quite everybody.

Little Miss Late was laying in bed worrying about whether her Christmas letter had arrived in time. And then in the distance she heard the tinkle of sleigh bells.

Little Miss Late jumped out of bed and ran to the window, just in time to see a sleigh and eight tiny reindeer swoop low over her garden.

She knew in an instant it must be Father Christmas.

She held her breath and listened.

The sleigh disappeared out of sight, the tinkle of bells faded ...

… And then grew stronger as Father Christmas and Mr Christmas circled over Little Miss Late's house and glided to a halt on her roof! She heard the patter of little hoofs, the sound of heavy footsteps above her head and knew the letter had arrived in time!

Little Miss Late dashed down to her living room …

… Just as Father Christmas and Mr Christmas emerged from the fireplace.

Father Christmas was dressed all in red from his head to his foot with a bundle of toys on his back. He took a parcel from his sack and placed it in her stocking.

"And here is something for next year," said Mr Christmas, laying a present beside the Christmas tree. And then with a grin and a wink they disappeared back up the chimney. Little Miss Late looked at the present Mr Christmas had left her.

Can you guess what it was?

It was an advent calendar to help her remember when to post her letter to Father Christmas next year!

MR. MEN
12 Days of Christmas

Now, you and I know that Christmas is in the winter, in December, the 25th of December to be exact.

Mr Muddle on the other hand is not like you and I.

He does not know when Christmas is. In fact Mr Muddle has never got it right.

For instance, last year he gave Mr Lazy a football for Christmas … on the 25th of July. In the middle of the summer!

He can never get the right day or the right present for that matter.

But Mr Muddle had a plan. A plan to make sure that this Christmas he would get the right day.

So on the 25th of January, Mr Muddle went to see Mr Messy.

"Happy Christmas," he announced, giving him a brand new bath.
The wrong day. And the wrong present if Mr Messy was honest, but
Mr Muddle had a plan and he was going to stick to it.

On the 25th of February he gave Little Miss Tiny a new pair of shoes.

The wrong day and the wrong size!

On the 25th of March he gave Mr Grumpy a joke book.

Mr Grumpy thought he must be joking.

On the 25th of April, Mr Muddle gave Little Miss Quick a pet tortoise.

"He's not very quick off the mark," observed Little Miss Quick.

On the 25th of May he gave Mr Bump a skateboard.

OUCH!

On the 25th of June he gave Mr Tickle a skipping rope.

What a tangle!

On the 25th of July he gave Little Miss Sunshine an umbrella.

I don't think she'll be needing that!

On the 25th of August, Mr Muddle gave Mr Quiet a drum kit.

Mr Noisy was very jealous.

On the 25th of September he gave the Little Miss Twins one pair of socks.

"Oh, too kind," said the Twins.

On the 25th of October he gave Little Miss Whoops a china vase.

WHOOPS!

On the 25th of November, Mr Muddle gave Mr Slow a sports car.

"Heeeeelp!"

Mr Muddle had been wrong eleven times. So when he got up on the 25th of December, his twelfth day of Christmas, he was sure he must have the right day.

He took a Christmas pudding round to his neighbour and knocked on his door.

"Happy Christmas!" Mr Muddle announced proudly, to his friend.

"I think you're in a muddle, Mr Muddle. It can't be Christmas because I'm off on my summer holiday!" said …

... Mr Wrong!

MR. MEN

A Christmas Pantomime

Little Miss Trouble is a real handful.

A real handful of trouble.

And there is no time when she is more of a handful than at Christmas.

There are just so many chances for Little Miss Trouble to cause trouble.

Last Christmas, Little Miss Trouble pinched a slice of Little Miss Neat's Christmas cake and blamed it on Mr Greedy.

Little Miss Neat was not very happy with Mr Greedy.

She told Little Miss Splendid that Mr Quiet had said she looked like a Christmas tree in that hat.

Little Miss Splendid was not very happy with Mr Quiet.

And Little Miss Trouble sent Mr Chatterbox a huge gobstopper pretending it was a Christmas present from Little Miss Chatterbox.

Needless to say, the Chatterboxes' Christmas was not as chatty as usual.

So when it came to the auditions for Little Miss Bossy's Christmas pantomime, Aladdin, it will come as no surprise to hear that she did not get a part.

"I know what you're like," said Little Miss Bossy, "you'll just be trouble from start to finish!"

Little Miss Trouble went home in a foul mood.

"Trouble," she muttered to herself. "I'll show her trouble."

Little Miss Bossy was very pleased with the rest of the auditions.

Little Miss Star got the part of Aladdin, Little Miss Sunshine was to play the Princess, Mr Mean would be the Evil Wizard, Mr Small the Genie of the Lamp and Mr Grumpy, a perfect Widow Twankey.

However, Little Miss Bossy was not so pleased once rehearsals got under way.

Someone put itching powder in Widow Twankey's wig.

Someone told the Princess that Aladdin had said she wasn't pretty
enough to be a princess.

Someone put an egg in the Evil Wizard's curly slipper.

Someone glued the lid of the magic lamp shut and the Genie could not get out.

And someone put a mouse in Aladdin's cave and Aladdin proved to be less brave than everyone had assumed.

It was a disaster.

And Little Miss Bossy knew exactly why it had been a disaster. That evening she went round to Little Miss Trouble's house.

"Okay, I give up," said Little Miss Bossy. "You can have a part in the pantomime."

"Truly?" said Little Miss Trouble. "Which part?"

"Just turn up on the opening night and you'll find out," replied Little Miss Bossy.

On the opening night of the pantomime, Little Miss Trouble was so excited that she barely knew what to do with herself.

She turned up early to discover which part she was to play.

Little Miss Trouble couldn't wait to see her costume.

Just before the start of the performance, Little Miss Bossy called the cast together.

"I thought Little Miss Trouble was going to be here tonight," said Little Miss Sunshine.

"Oh, she is," said Little Miss Bossy.

"Where is she?" asked Mr Mean, looking around the dressing room.

Little Miss Bossy grinned.

"Over here," came a muffled reply from the back of the pantomime horse.

"Keep still!" said Little Miss Stubborn at the front.

MR. MEN
A White Christmas

Father Christmas, as you might imagine, is very busy just before Christmas. And one of the jobs that keeps him busy is reading everyone's Christmas letters.

Last year, he received a letter from a little boy in Australia who had a very special wish. He wished for a white Christmas.

Now, as you might or might not know, it is very hot at Christmas time in Australia. And because it is very hot at Christmas, it never snows.

"Hmm," said Father Christmas to himself. "Now, who would be the best person to help me with this wish?"

And so it was that Mr Snow received a visit from Father Christmas.

"Hello, Mr Snow," said Father Christmas. "I have a job for you. A little boy in Australia called Ben has asked for a white Christmas. Do you think you can make his wish come true?"

"I think I know just the person who can," said Mr Snow, after a moment's thought.

"Excellent!" said Father Christmas. "You can borrow my sleigh. It's a rather long walk to Australia!"

Mr Snow packed his suitcase and set off for Australia.

On the way he picked up a very good friend of his, Little Miss Magic.
It took them no time at all to get to Australia in Father Christmas's sleigh.

Ben was very excited when he saw Mr Snow and Little Miss Magic standing on his doorstep.

"Hello, Ben," said Little Miss Magic. "We're here to make your wish come true."

"I think we need to hurry up," said Mr Snow. "I'm starting to melt!"

So Little Miss Magic muttered some very magic words and suddenly
the temperature dropped, huge grey clouds rolled over the horizon,
and it began to snow.

Ben could not believe his eyes.

It snowed.

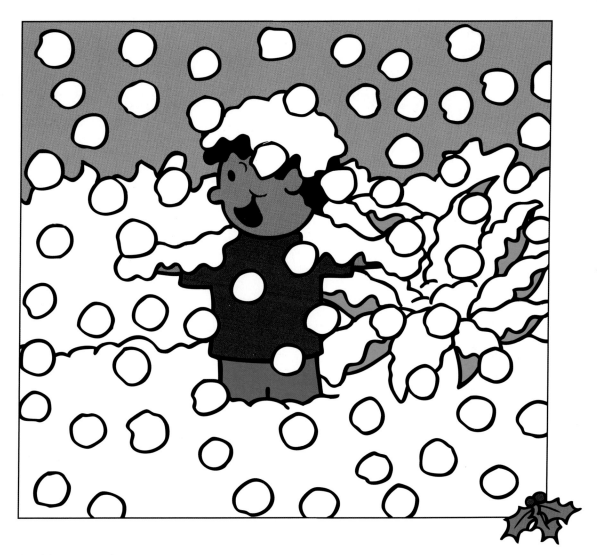

And it snowed.

And it snowed.

Everywhere was covered in a thick blanket of fluffy, white snow.

Ben ran inside his house and put on all his jumpers.

"Would you like to come for a ride in Father Christmas's flying sleigh?" asked Mr Snow.

"Yes please!" said Ben.

They climbed aboard and Mr Snow took off.

Ben looked in wonder at the snowy landscape below them.

But everywhere they went Ben began to notice the same thing.

The kangaroos, standing in the snowy outback, did not look very happy.

The crocodiles in the icy river did not look very happy.

And everyone on the snowy beach did not look very happy.

They looked very unhappy and very cold.

"Oh dear," sighed Ben. "I don't think anyone else wants the snow as much as I do. I think you'd better make it all go away."

So Little Miss Magic muttered some more very magic words and before you could say, "Hey Presto" the clouds had rolled away and the sun came out and melted all the snow.

Ben looked sadly at the puddles at his feet. And it was then that Mr Snow had an idea. "Why don't we fly to places where people do like snow?"

"Can we?" cried Ben.

"We certainly can," said Little Miss Magic.

And so they did just that.

They flew to Coldland and went sledging with Mr Sneeze.

Then they visited Mr Bump and went ice skating.

"Do you know where they have more snow than anywhere else?"
Mr Snow asked.

"Where?" asked Ben.

"At the North Pole!" said Mr Snow.

"That's where Father Christmas lives!" cried Ben.

"Indeed it is," said Mr Snow.

And that is how a little boy from Australia found himself at the North Pole in …

… a snowball fight with Mr Snow, Little Miss Christmas, Mr Christmas and Father Christmas!

And what a snowball fight it was!

"I'm sorry you didn't get to have a white Christmas in Australia," laughed Mr Snow, as his snowball hit Father Christmas's chest.

"But at least you did get to see one white Christmas …"

"... a white Father Christmas! We've turned him into a snowman!"

MR. MEN
Meet Father Christmas

It was Christmas Eve and Little Miss Tiny was excited.

And the more she thought about Christmas, the more excited she became.

Very, very excited!

"I wonder what Father Christmas is doing at this moment," she thought to herself. "He might be polishing his sleigh … he might be feeding his reindeer … or he might be wrapping presents. He might even be wrapping MY present! I do wish I could visit him and see."

Just then, she heard somebody outside her mousehole.

That's right, Little Miss Tiny is so tiny she lives in a mousehole, in the skirting board, in the dining room, in Home Farm.

It was Mr Daydream. "I was on my way to see Father Christmas," he said. "Would you like to come along on a Christmas holiday with me?"

Little Miss Tiny could not believe her luck.

If it really was luck.

Waiting outside was Mr Daydream's magic bird.

Mr Daydream's enormous, yellow, magic bird.

Enormous to you or I, but as big as the moon to Little Miss Tiny.

Mr Daydream and Little Miss Tiny climbed onto its back and off they flew to the North.

North all the way to the North Pole.

"Look, there's a house with an upside down roof," said Little Miss Tiny as they flew on.

"Where are we?" she asked.

"We are flying over Muddleland," said Mr Daydream. "Would you like to have a look?"

"Yes please," said Little Miss Tiny.

In Muddleland everything is in a muddle and Christmas time is no exception.

In Muddleland they don't decorate their Christmas trees, they decorate their furniture.

In Muddleland they don't have Christmas lunch, they have Christmas breakfast.

And in Muddleland they don't hang Christmas stockings, they hang gloves above their fireplaces!

And then they were off again, and before long they found themselves flying over Cleverland.

Now as you can well imagine everyone in Cleverland is clever.

Even the sheep are clever.

So clever, in fact, that they celebrate Christmas.

Little Miss Tiny and Mr Daydream stopped off at many places on their way to the North Pole.

In Loudland, they heard the loudest carol singers in the world.

They were much too loud for Little Miss Tiny.

And they flew to Nonsenseland, where the snow is yellow!

"Just one more stop before we get to the North Pole," announced Mr Daydream, finally.

"Where is that?" asked Little Miss Tiny.

"Coldland!"

And it was. Cold, that is. Very, very, very cold.

And in Coldland they had tea with Mr Sneeze.

ATISHOO!!! sneezed Mr Sneeze.

ATISHOO! sneezed Little Miss Tiny.

"Oh dear," said Mr Daydream. "I think you might have caught a cold."

At last they reached the North Pole. Little Miss Tiny couldn't wait to meet Father Christmas. But where was he?

They landed beside a large chimney stack standing all on its own.

"How odd," said Little Miss Tiny.

Suddenly there was a rumbling sound and two big, black boots appeared in the fireplace.

"I think I need to lose a bit of weight," echoed a voice from the chimney. It was Father Christmas doing chimney practice with Mr Christmas!

And with a **POP** Father Christmas squeezed out of the chimney, covered in soot.

"Hello, there," he boomed to Little Miss Tiny. "How about a big tour for a little person? I've got to clean myself up, but Mr Christmas will show you round."

"Yes please," said Little Miss Tiny.

ATISHOO! she sneezed.

"Bless you," said Mr Christmas and Father Christmas together.

Mr Christmas led Little Miss Tiny into a large log cabin where she met the elves who were making all the toys.

ATISHOO! sneezed Little Miss Tiny.

"Bless you, bless you, bless you," chorused the elves.

159

Then Mr Christmas took Little Miss Tiny to feed Father Christmas' reindeer.

"Rudolf has a cold just like your one," said Mr Christmas.

ATISHOO! sneezed Rudolf.

"Bless you," said Little Miss Tiny.

And best of all they saw where all the presents were stored.

"And this one," said Mr Christmas, picking up a very tiny parcel, "is yours."

Little Miss Tiny's face lit up with excitement.

"It may be small," said Mr Christmas. "But Father Christmas won't forget to deliver it tonight."

And just then Father Christmas popped his head around the corner. He had dusted off his suit and it was bright red again. He was ready for his busy night.

Little Miss Tiny let out a small yawn. It was getting very late for a little person.

So Little Miss Tiny and Mr Daydream said goodbye to Father Christmas, Mr Christmas, the reindeer and the elves and climbed back on the enormous yellow bird. Little Miss Tiny could hardly keep her eyes open as they flew all the way home.

On Christmas morning, Little Miss Tiny woke to find herself sitting in her armchair, in her mousehole, in the skirting board, in the dining room, in Home Farm.

There, next to her tiny pinecone tree, was a parcel. Father Christmas had been!

"Gosh," she said to herself. "Did that Christmas holiday really happen?

Maybe it was just a dream?"

But then …

ATISHOO! she sneezed.

MR. MEN
The Christmas Tree

Mr Forgetful had forgotten to buy a Christmas tree.

Can you imagine?

No Christmas tree!

Where would Father Christmas put the Christmas presents?

Normally Mr Happy helps Mr Forgetful to buy his tree, but this year Mr Happy had gone away for Christmas.

And now it was too late.

All the Christmas trees had been sold.

Everyone else had a tree.

Mr Greedy had bought his tree.

Mr Skinny had bought his tree.

Mr Mean had bought his tree.

And Mr Nonsense had bought six, just in case he ran out.

What nonsense!

Even Little Miss Late had a tree, although she had bought the last one left.

Mr Forgetful realised that he had no choice but to go into the forest and cut down his own tree.

So, he set off through the snow.

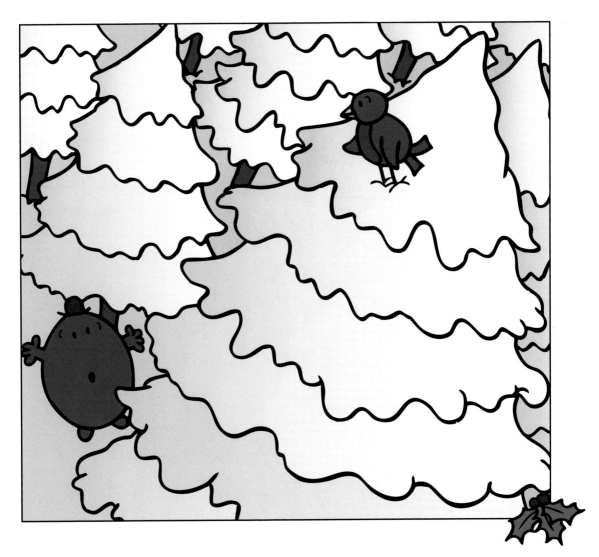

Mr Forgetful walked and walked.

And walked some more.

But he could not find the perfect tree he was looking for.

They were too twisted.

Or too spindly.

Or too big.

"That won't fit in my living room," muttered Mr Forgetful.

After much searching he finally found a tree that was just right.

And it was then he realised he had forgotten his saw.

"Bother!" he said to himself. "I'll have to go back for it."

And it was then he realised that he had forgotten the way home!

Poor Mr Forgetful.

As he wandered through the forest trying to find his way home, he came upon some footprints in the snow.

"These must be my footprints," he guessed. "And if I follow them they should lead me back home."

But being the forgetful fellow he is, he forgot to follow them backwards and followed them forwards.

Back to the Christmas tree he had found!

Mr Forgetful was now in a terrible muddle.

As I'm sure you are. I know I am.

And he was cold.

And it was getting dark.

So he climbed a tree to see if he could see his house, but all he could see were trees.

And more trees.

In desperation he cried for help. **"HELP!"**

And as luck would have it, help was at hand.

Help in the form of Father Christmas who was flying over the forest in his sleigh at that very moment.

"I was just on my way to deliver your present to your house," said Father Christmas. "Would you like a lift?

"By the way," asked Father Christmas, once they had arrived, "what were you doing up a tree in the middle of a forest on Christmas Eve?"

"You know what?" said Mr Forgetful. "I can't remember!"

"Now, where shall I put this?" asked Father Christmas, pulling a parcel out of his sack. A Christmas tree shaped parcel.

"Well I never," said Mr. Forgetful, suddenly remembering. "You are a marvel!"

Which just goes to show that Father Christmas really does know what everyone wants for Christmas.

Even if they've forgotten it themselves!